APR 3 0 2015
W9-BZU-100

The Wren and the Sparrow

To my mother and the memory of my father —J.P.L.

To the memory of my grandparents. — Y.N.

KAR-BEN PUBLISHING
A division of Lerner Publishing Group, Inc.
241 First Avenue North
Minneapolis, MN 55401 USA
1-800-4-KARBEN

Website address: www.karben.com

Main body text set in Oldbook ITC Std. 16/22.
Typeface provided by International Typeface Corp.

Photo credit page 31: © Galerie Bilderwelt/Hulton Archive/Getty Images

Library of Congress Cataloging-in-Publication Data

Lewis, J. Patrick.
The Wren and the Sparrow / by J. Patrick Lewis ; illustrated by Yevgenia Nayberg
pages cm.
Summary: An allegorical tale about Nazi occupied Poland in which a town's residents are forced to turn over their musical instruments. A young student rescues the hurdy-gurdy of her teacher, who has presumably befallen a terrible fate, and later, a young boy finds the instrument and intends to pass it—and the importance of remembering—on to his future grandchildren"—Provided by publisher.
ISBN 978-1-4677-1951-3 (lib. bdg. : alk. paper)
1. Holocaust, Jewish (1939-1945)—Poland—Lodz—Juvenile fiction. [1. Holocaust, Jewish (1939-1945)—Poland—Lodz—Fiction. 2. Holocaust survivors--Fiction. 3. Jews--Poland--Fiction. 4. Allegories.] I. Cimatoribus, Alessandra, illustrator. II. Title.
PZ7.L5866Wr 2014
[Fic]—dc23 2013021757

Manufactured in the United States of America
1 – VI – 7/15/14

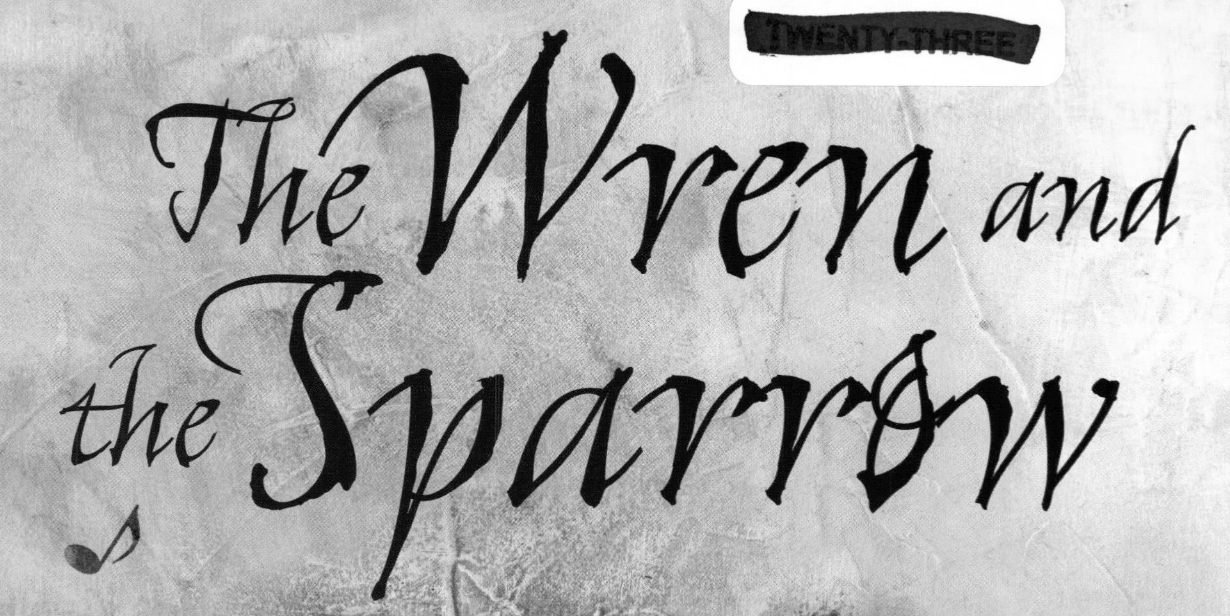

The Wren and the Sparrow

J. Patrick Lewis

Illustrated by **Yevgenia Nayberg**

KAR-BEN PUBLISHING

In a dark time, the Old Man lived in shadows. A weaver of carpets, he spent his days at a loom and his nights singing to a hurdy-gurdy, the only thing he owned.

He sang so beautifully that it must have amused the stars, they twinkled so. His neighbors called him the Wren. The Wren had one beloved student, a young girl known only as the Sparrow.

The town, a little hamlet in the center of Poland, hung on the edge of despair, not far from the Tyrant and his guards.

Magpies gasped and crows caw-cawtioned at what they saw from the sky. No bird nested in a land without trees. The trees had all been cut down for kindling.

Food and clothing were strictly rationed. Stores that once provided necessities were boarded up. Voices of protest, long silenced, were but a memory. The town shriveled up like a rose without rain.

Once, many years ago, music could be heard in the streets at all hours. But the gift of music soon dwindled to a sigh.

On a day that shamed the sky, people were herded into the center of the town and forced to hand over their musical instruments—wooden or metal, it made no difference—to the Tyrant's guards who carelessly pitched them into wagons.

A six-year-old's only possession, ten finger cymbals, tinkled like the sound of spring escaping winter. The guards held the boy upside down and shook him until the cymbals fell from his hands.

The marketplace groaned when a battered pipe organ was wheeled in a cart to the graveyard of musical instruments. The heart of the town's symphony stopped beating.

Then, from two blocks away, a melody arrived in a velvet coach. "It's the Wren!" someone whispered.

"He must be crazy in the head. The Wren would never give up his hurdy-gurdy."

But there he was, in his wooden shoes, tattered black suit, and woolen cap. He nodded to the Sparrow and shook with fear for what he was about to do.

“Your rattle-box,” the guard demanded. “Hand it over.”

“Allow an old man one last song,” said the Wren. Only the few who stood next to him could hear him murmur, “. . . so that no one will ever forget this day.”

Without waiting for an answer, he began to play. Slowly, softly at first, the crowd hummed, then joined in the singing.

Before long the marketplace, the entire town seemed to shake with song.

It is our grief It is our pain It is our fate,

We don't complain.

Our hopeless days Give way to nights

Whose wounded stars

Have dimmed their lights.

The words pierced the Polish sky, releasing the rain. "Look, Sparrow, look!" shouted the Old Man. "Even the clouds are weeping." And the song of the singers—one people, one voice—rose and sank and rose again against the will of the evil Tyrant.

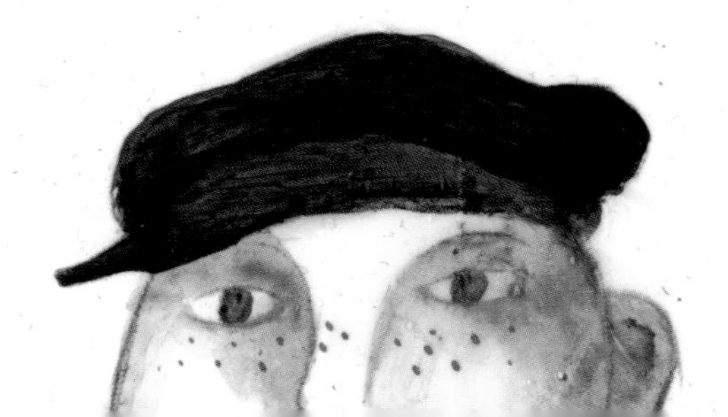

The guard ripped the stringed organ from the Old Man's hands, but he would not stop singing. As the Wren was being dragged away, he sang, louder and louder, his last song on earth.

Then he was gone.

The day sealed itself into the lockbox of memory.

Later that night, the musical instruments were piled high next to the old button factory. They would be taken outside the barbed wire the next day, and destroyed.

Ducking under the window lights, the Sparrow sneaked up to one of the wagons, found what she was looking for, and made off with it in the darkness. Somehow, she felt the Wren watching over her.

During the long nightmare, people buried their most precious belongings, like the last little pieces of themselves, in basements, attics and walls. The Sparrow tucked the hurdy-gurdy behind a boiler in the basement of her apartment building, where it lay undiscovered.

And so it was that she kept the Wren's legacy alive.

Three years later, when the tyranny became too much for the world to bear, the Tyrant was overthrown, and his ruthlessness died with him.

One day, a small boy, one of the few children to survive, was scavenging for scraps of food when he found the hurdy-gurdy behind the basement boiler.

He shouted to his friend to come quickly, and as they poked at it and strummed its strings, a piece of butcher paper slipped out from under the cracked soundboard.

The boy thrilled to the message, as if it were a note in a bottle floating at sea.

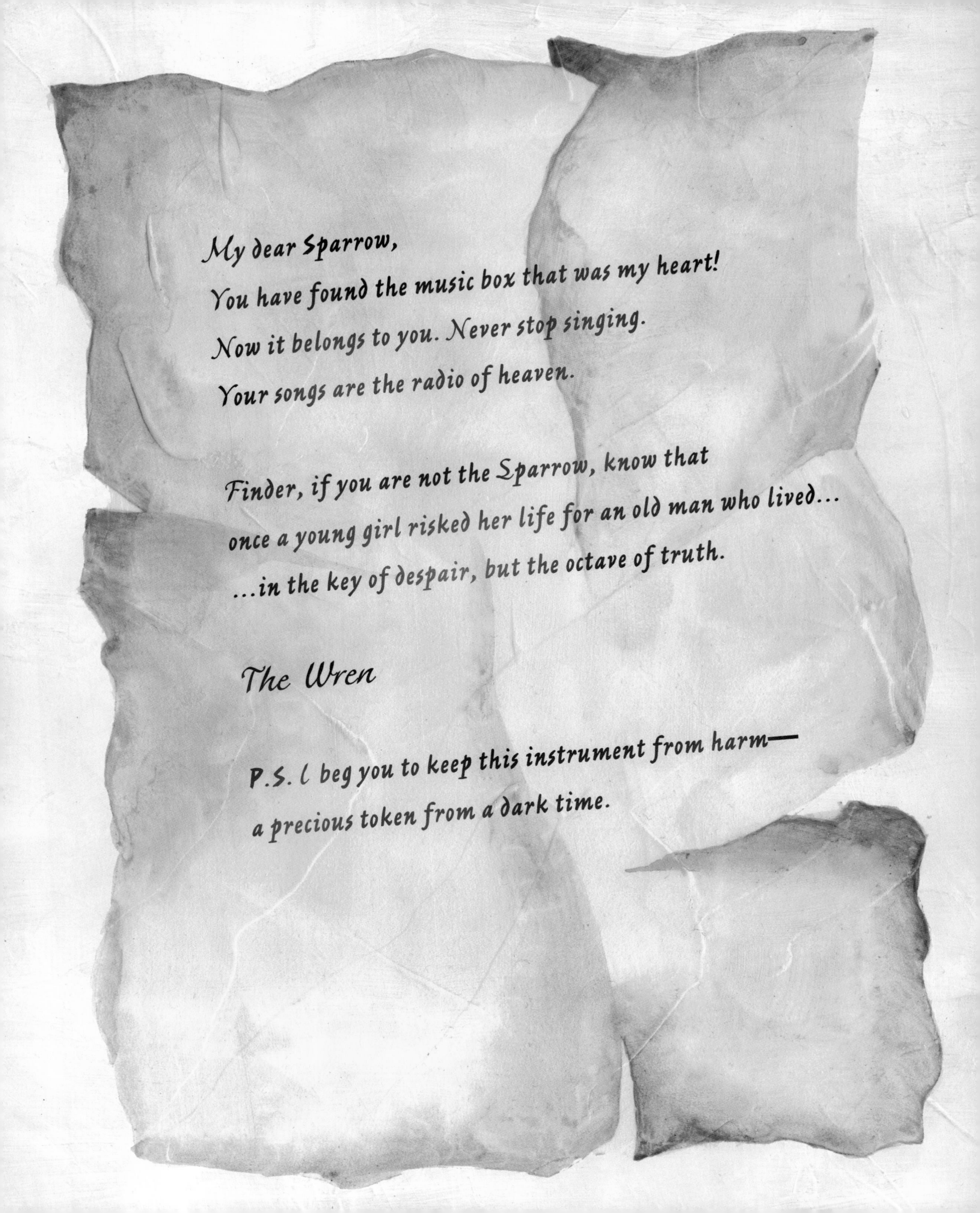

My dear Sparrow,
You have found the music box that was my heart!
Now it belongs to you. Never stop singing.
Your songs are the radio of heaven.

Finder, if you are not the Sparrow, know that
once a young girl risked her life for an old man who lived...
...in the key of despair, but the octave of truth.

The Wren

P.S. I beg you to keep this instrument from harm—
a precious token from a dark time.

The boy did just that. The hurdy-gurdy, safe from the axe and the flame, went with him everywhere—

—from Poland

to France,

and finally to America.

The music box began to show signs of age.

Through the years, so did the boy, who grew into an old man . . .

. . . the old man I am now. Soon I will keep the promise I made to the Wren I never knew, and hide a note in the Sparrow's music box for my great-grandchildren to find . . .

. . . so that no one will ever forget.

Afterword

This story is a work of imagination inspired by the street performers of the Lodz Ghetto. In the city of Lodz, as in Jewish communities throughout Europe during the Holocaust, the Jews were rounded up and packed into a fenced section of Lodz, which became known as the Lodz Ghetto.

In 1940, the Lodz Ghetto, one of the largest ghettos in Europe, held 230,000 people. In 1945, when the Soviet Army liberated the city from the Nazis, fewer than 1000 of Lodz's Jewish community had survived.

Music was part of ghetto life, helping to sustain the spirits of the Jewish community in those dark days. Street performers, including children, sang or played music in exchange for a coin, a bit of food, or often nothing at all. Yankele Hershkowitz was one such street performer in the Lodz Ghetto. Like the Wren, he resisted the Nazis with his songs, offering a glimmer of a better world.

As in this story, some of the musical instruments played in the ghettos and concentration camps survived the Holocaust; most of their owners did not. But their music inspired both grown-ups and children in the ghettos to believe that, even in the bleak world of the Shoah, beauty and hope for humanity still lived.

A Jewish boy playing a violin in the Warsaw ghetto, Poland, February 1941.

About the Author and Illustrator

J. Patrick Lewis has published over eighty-five children's picture and poetry books with Creative Editions, National Geographic, Knopf, Atheneum, Dial, Chronicle Books, Candlewick, Harcourt, Little, Brown, Scholastic, DK Ink, Holiday House, Sleeping Bear Press, and others. He received the NCTE Excellence in Children's Poetry Award, and was the Poetry Foundation's third U.S. Children's Poet Laureate (2011-2013).

Yevgenia Nayberg is an award-winning illustrator, painter and stage designer. A native of Kiev, Ukraine, she graduated from The National School of Arts. Yevgenia's paintings have been featured in solo exhibitions in New York City, Miami, Los Angeles and Moscow. She has designed sets and costumes for over 40 theatrical productions and received a number of prestigious awards for her stage designs. Her illustrations have appeared in magazines and children's books as well as on album covers, book covers and theatre posters.